THE GIRL I MET IN BANGKOK

NOLEEN C. GEORGE

These short stories are works of fiction based around actual events. Names, characters, organisations, places, events and incidents have been changed to protect the identities of the women involved.

Some themes contain sexually explicit content, adult language, and other content that may be offensive to some readers. Please ensure that underage people do not access the content.

Dedication

This book is dedicated to all the amazing, strong, intelligent, beautiful and unstoppable women, girlfriends, wives, and mothers I have met in Bangkok. May your stories inspire and motivate anyone that finds themselves trapped by circumstances, finances, and situations beyond their control.

May these stories show women all around the globe that we are a force to be reckoned with, and we will survive and thrive through anything that life throws at us.

No woman ever needs to feel alone in their struggles, none of us needs to do it all alone, and none of us needs to settle for second best. We can do it all, have it all, and we have a tribe of women around us to help each other get it all.

Just knowing, meeting or sharing a moment with the women in Bangkok has inspired me to be better, to do better, and to give more.

This book is for all the fantastic, energetic, strong, amazing, feisty, vivacious, independent, successful, adventurous, and beautiful women I have met in Bangkok.

Kob Khun Ka. (*Thank you*)

The place I call home

"The secret of change is to focus all of your energy, not on fighting the old, but on building the new."
– SOCRATES

Bangkok, the city of light. The city of love, angels, Buddha, and every hedonistic delight you can imagine or afford. However, it is also the city of bitterness, darkness, and loneliness. This town can open its arms and embrace you into the fold like a long lost daughter or son. However, if you are of the sort that is not strong-willed enough or if you don't have the openness of mind and heart that this city demands, it will chew you up and spit you out. I have seen both sides, and I have lived both sides.

Expats flock to Bangkok for a myriad of reasons. Generally, there are two types of Bangkok ex-pats. Firstly, the one running away from something. Secondly, the one running towards something. I have met both types, and I have a foot firmly placed on either side of the spectrum.

A few years ago, I found myself in the unenviable position of being alone, confused and without options, possibilities, or prospects.

The situation was all the worst as I had limited resources, clarification of mind or motivation to change any of it. For the first time in my life, I honestly and comprehensively understood what "down and out" meant. I was so depressed that I could not see straight. When your future is bleak, there is very little else you can see around you except despair, gloom and darkness. The number of genuinely terrible decisions I made during that time still haunts me. I knew with every fibre of my being that something had to change, but I was incapable of figuring out how I could even begin to do that. The proverbial light at the end of the tunnel came in the way of a friend offering a new start and reaching out a hand to help lift me out of the swamp that became my life. He, at the time, had no idea what I was going through and that his email was like a beacon of hope, a light at the end of a dark tunnel.

My ex-neighbour had moved to Thailand ten years before receiving his email. I reached out to him, asking what life was like in Thailand and what opportunities Thailand offered. At that time, I had no intention of moving to Thailand, and my motivation was pure curiosity. The response I got was a bit jarring and somewhat surprising, "Come on over, I will you get settled and make sure you are comfortable. Opportunities are here if you are willing and able to recognise it and take it," he wrote.

"Really?" I replied. "What sort of opportunities? I am intrigued." The word 'opportunity' rang in my ears like a chapel bell. It was what I needed, an opportunity, was what I craved; it was what my soul was crying out for, and I knew it would lift me out of the darkness and gloom that always surrounded me. I quickly sent him a direct text to get more information and to settle my curiosity.

"Tell me more about these opportunities, please. It sounds like something I need," my text read.

"Well, for one, you can teach English. There is always a great need for English teachers here."

"That sounds great, but I've not taught before. Will I need some experience?"

"Experience you can get when you are here. Do some research on TEFL courses offered in Thailand; some of them offer practical classroom hours. You can use that as experience and look for a temporary teaching job in Bangkok." It all sounded too good to be true.

You won't be amiss in assuming I jumped at the opportunity, but that was not the case. I ruminated on it for months, placing obstacles in my path. Making ridiculous deals with myself, indulging in useless self-bargaining. I would often tell myself things such as, "I will do a TEFL course first and then go." Or, I would find myself thinking, "First drop three kilograms and then you will be ready to leave." All the while, knowing full well the dealing and bargaining were all useless and time-wasting procrastination. I was scared at the prospect of packing up my life, leaving everything I knew and, in a sense, abandoning all my comfort zones. Irrespective of how uncomfortable those zones had become, it was still familiar and secure.

Driving to work one day, the conversation in my head changed. Instead of the bargains and negotiations, I started listing all the reasons I should stay. I came up with one – my family. Under reasons to leave, I came up with ten. Clearly, you would say to yourself; I had a no-brainer on my hands. The ten reasons tumbled around my brain all day. I could barely focus on work. The ruminating went on for weeks until I finally had had enough.

It was just after the lunch break when a colleague made a simple request that was work-related. I can no longer recall what it was exactly, but it was in no way rude, or negative but something about the request rubbed me up the wrong way. My colleague had a very abrupt way of communicating, and at that moment, her brashness made every other pain point in my life slice like a katana. All I recall is feeling the anger well up in me. It felt like a fireball starting in the pit of my stomach and worked its way to my throat. I pushed my chair away from my desk, marched into the Director's office and said, "Thank you for this opportunity, Dave. It's been a great experience, but I am here now to tell you that I am leaving. I will tender my resignation by the end of the day. I am moving to Bangkok,"

"OK, that sounds great. How much time would you like to take off? I am sure we can arrange it for you." Dave said.

"No, Dave. You misunderstood. I am moving to Bangkok. I do not plan on returning for at least a year – if ever. I am resigning." I had to repeat it.

Admittedly and understandably, Dave was not very happy about it as I had just started the job six months ago. As loyal as I am, there was no way I was going to lose my sanity because someone I hardly knew appointed me a job. At that moment, I knew beyond doubt what I needed to do. Other than the ten reasons I had thought of that one morning and hadn't stopped thinking about, I had to do it for peace of mind, my sanity and dignity, because steadily I was losing all the longer I stayed in Cape Town.

I resigned that day. I went home that evening and broke the news to my family. I was half expecting drama and a struggle of words, but no such thing happened. Their only question was, "Why, Bangkok?" A valid question considering they didn't know that much about the city and

I never mentioned it before. Luckily, the answer and reason were simple. I knew one person there, and it was the one place I could think of that offered me the change I so desperately needed. My family was comfortable with the fact that I would not be alone, and they knew the person I was going to stay with very well. No matter your age, your parents will always think of you as a child.

The funniest question came from my sister, "Why are you moving to a third world country?" We all burst out laughing at that. A strange question when you consider that Africa is known and fills the political definition of a third world continent. I had to clarify it for her and said, "They are not a third world country. We are. Thailand is just Asian. It's different from what we know, that's all. And that is what I need the most, a huge change. A change everything." My sister mulled it over for a few minutes and then simply shrugged her shoulders, and that was the end of her inquiry or interest.

A month later, I was on a plane heading to Bangkok. All I had was a suitcase filled with my best summer clothes, a head filled with dreams of island living and a great desire for change. My first week in Bangkok went by in a flurry. I landed the Monday, Tuesday I had a job interview to fill the position as a kindergarten teacher, by Wednesday I was working. Thursday, I was looking for an apartment, and by

.urday, I had moved in and started my life in Bangkok. In a big city like Bangkok, I was pleasantly surprised by how quickly you can make friends. I managed to secure myself a small but feisty, funny, and loyal group of friends. It becomes apparent very quickly that as an ex-pat, you find commonalities with people easily as you all have the same basic goals and one common element of being an ex-pat.

I fell in love with everything in and around Bangkok - the good, the great, the bad and even the worst. It was as if everything I went through in Cape Town had prepared me for my life in a vibrant and sometimes complicated city. I took to Bangkok like a long lost native that has finally returned. I have now called Bangkok home for many years. My Bangkok adventure has been an incredible journey and an adventure that continues almost daily.

All those years ago, when I packed my belongings in a backpack and headed to a city I did not know, the only motivation I had was the urgent need for change. I needed to see something different, hear something different, smell something different, taste something different, feel something different, and more importantly – be someone different. From day one, Bangkok did not disappoint. I didn't only meet a girl in Bangkok; I met the woman I am today.

With living in Bangkok, I realised that I no longer run away from a future or have no vision to see one that I want to create for myself. Instead, I run towards my future, and I am constantly challenging myself to strive for the best possible future. These days I am a far cry from the girl who was once absorbed in self-loathing and cloaked in sadness. I find myself tackling my unstoppable ambition with vigour. I embrace every obstacle and challenge that comes my way. I no longer shirk from challenges, whether physical or emotive and I no longer cringe from those that would have me think I am less than what I am. Moving to Bangkok has encouraged me to live my best life possible. To live it my way and on my terms. Back home, I shied away from challenges because I didn't have the emotional or mental strength to deal with anything in a mature, calm and efficient manner. Now, managing, dealing, and overcoming has become second nature.

After delving into the teaching profession for a few years, I decided to pursue a career in freelance writing. My writing career has given me so much in terms of career satisfaction. The vibrancy of Bangkok feeds my energy to meet clients, negotiate deals, write to deadline, deliver assignments, and hustle every day to make a life of which I am proud and one that I love.

I can do what I love and split my time between Cape Town and Bangkok – the two cities I love. My new chosen career has allowed me to travel through South East Asia extensively. I have been lucky to see and experience many different cultures and traditions. My life has become so rich, and I can't imagine trading it in for anything.

The city of Bangkok has given me so much, and I hope to give equally in return. It has shown me nothing but love, and I love it in return. For now, I can't imagine living, loving, and thriving anywhere else in the world. Bangkok is my home.

Thailand changed the way I love

"Friendship means understanding, not agreement. It means forgiveness, not forgetting. It means the memories last, even if contact is lost."
– UNKNOWN

I gave up on finding my soul mate after a failed marriage and a few failed relationships. Love and relationships left me jaded and somewhat cynical. The widely held belief that there is one person out there who can make your soul sing or who is the perfect fit for you was absurd to me.

Now you might think that this is a love story. A story about how I found my life long partner and how we are blissfully on the road to our happily ever after. It is in a manner, but nothing to what you may consider familiar. I have indeed found great love and the right partner, but there is nothing romantic about our relationship. This story is not about the 'friend zone' either.

I met Emily on a nine-hour road trip from Bangkok to Laos. It was not 'love' at first sight but rather a tangled mess of preconceived notions, misinterpretations, and total confusion of intentions. At first glance, I thought Emily was Japanese and that she could not speak a word of English. She thought I was a bombastic attention seeker desperate for friends.

The truth, we found out later, was that Emily's nationality is Chinese-Russian mix and speaks perfect English. Her quiet and shy demeanour is due to her preference for observing her surroundings without drawing any attention to herself. I am certainly not bombastic. Talkative, yes, and I won't go so far as to call myself an extrovert, but I do enjoy a good, intelligent conversation and to meet new people.

Emily and I did not exchange much in the way of pleasantries or talk during that nine-hour road trip. I prefer to sleep and listen to music on long journeys, and she prefers to do the same. When we got to Laos, we got caught up in the task at hand, which was to get a six-month tourist visa to further our stay in and exploration of Thailand. The queue that seems never to end, the heat and confusion experienced at embassy offices around the world, do not inspire or enthuse you to start up conversations or indulge in pleasantries with fellow travellers. Once we got all the necessary processes and procedures done, we and everyone else were far too tired and grumpy to engage in any conversation. All weary and slightly frustrated travellers made our way to the transport that would take us to the hotel. We all stumbled to our rooms, showered, slept, and rested weary bones.

To describe the hotel as 'nice' is an overstatement. And every time we returned there since, it has just steadily gotten worse. It can best be described as a ramshackle dinosaur desperately trying to cling to the last vestiges of grandeur it might have had some fifty or sixty years ago. The only way you can have a peaceful night's sleep there is if you are either dead tired or drunk On arrival, we were the first; later that evening, we were all uproariously the latter.

Then, later in the evening, rested and refreshed, all travelers slowly emerged from their rooms for dinner and drinks. On these trips, a little band of travelers usually form in the outside lobby sharing travel stories. Whether a seasoned traveler or a newbie, everyone has Thailand experiences and stories. When sharing these stories, beers, cigarettes, and all sorts of little snippets of life on the road, you quickly form a type of camaraderie.

People from every corner of the globe, all were having different dreams, aspirations and reasons for living in Thailand. We all spoke different languages, but all found commonality in the lifestyle of the traveller. It was then that I started talking to Emily, and as it turned out, we had much in common. We echoed each other's thoughts, sentiments, and narratives on life, love, and everything else. A trip that started dull and uneventful quickly took a turn for the better.

Everyone continued drinking, talking, and laughing until the wee hours of the morning. The outside lobby area of that little ramshackle hotel always became a hive of evening activity. Often by the end of the night, the bar fridge is empty and the ashtrays are overflowing. Emily proved to be entertaining and engaging company, and I found myself liking her a lot, as well as enjoying her company tremendously. We eventually crawled to our rooms in the early morning and went to sleep as restfully as the hotel elements allow. After copious bottles of beer, you thankfully become unaware of old hotel creaks and cracks, as well as any aspects of nature that choose to share your room. I was out like a light the second my head hit the faded white pillow.

The next day was the dreaded nine-hour return journey to Bangkok. And again, all the way, Emily and I had minimal contact. Sleep and hangover recovery were the primary objectives on that return trip. At the end of the trip, we said our goodbyes and promised to keep in touch. I left her company, not expecting that to happen. But true to her word, she did keep in touch, and a reunion meet up was quickly planned.

Since that meeting, Emily and I became close friends. We often shared text messages or phone calls sharing our Bangkok adventures. There was hardly a day that went by without any contact between the two of us. Our friendship soon developed into a deep, respectful, and understanding relationship.

That was how I met my soul mate, one of the most important people in my life, and how a girl from China and a girl from South Africa became the best of friends. Emily is my confidant, best friend, and in every sense of the term, my soul mate. No, we are not lovers, as some of you might try to guess but rather genuine and true friends.

Typically what we look for or need, and sometimes demand from lovers and life-partners, Emily has provided without request and conditions. Many of us have an all or nothing approach to the relationships we have in our lives. I know I did, as well. However, these days I take every relationship I have at its merits.

Relationships of any nature are never black and white; however, you can establish a solid basis with openness and understanding. I am not merely referring to getting to know someone but rather to establish a deep understanding of someone's motivations.

Previously, my relationships, romantic, and friendships were all based on what those relationships could do for me. Most of us spend half our lives looking for validation, and we expect the people we form connections with to provide it. These days, my view on relationships is to focus on how I can be a better me to bring value to someone else. It is hard, and a trial every day to be better than you were, but a journey and struggle well worth it. My friends back home have come to mean more to me. Their friendship strengthens me, emboldens me to take on any obstacles, and reinforces the ties that bind me to home. My friendship with Emily has taught me how to value my friendships forged over many years, how to recognise their expressions of love and how to be a better friend to them – even though I am over ten thousand kilometres away.

My views on love and relationships have changed drastically. Some may say that it is due to age and maturity, but I can't honestly give all the credit to maturity. The relationships I have fostered in Bangkok with people from different parts of the world, with people who have different cultural norms and traditions, these relationships have taught me how to look at how I develop relationships with people holistically, and not with a myopic view of what I experienced before.

I know of people that are my age or older who still follow the tried and tested when it comes to the relationships they have in their lives. These same people are constantly asking what went wrong when the relationship ends or sours. They don't realise that never changing, never learning and never looking towards themselves will always deliver the same result.

There is a twelve-year age difference between Emily and myself, but it matters little. She keeps me young, and I ground her. We laugh together, cry together, calm each other, and support each other. We have become each other's biggest cheerleaders and fans, as well as each other's sternest critics. We do not fear each other's honesty, and we do not shy away from sharing our brand of honesty. These elements of our friendship have made me realise that when people can't accept your quirks, your weird, your difficult, and your crazy, then they don't deserve to accept your best.

No, it is not all sunshine and roses, as we have had some major disagreements. However, it doesn't take a long time before we are apologising – whether we are right or wrong – laughing, crying, and reminding each other what absolute idiots we are. We recognise each other's differences and embrace them.

We have both since our Laos trip decided to make Bangkok our temporary home. And we are blissfully happy. We are actively pursuing our dreams and ambitions, we have found and lost loves, and through all of the ups and downs, we have been there for each other. Through the thick and thin and sometimes through the sick and the sin, we have been there for each other.

We are acutely aware that there will come a time when we are no longer going to be living in the same city or even in the same time zone. But for now, we don't focus on that; we just relish the time together and the time when we can be close enough to run to each other's aid when it is needed.

I am also highly aware that Emily may outgrow this friendship. Considering her age and the fact that I have been around long enough to know that people do not stay the same. Her needs, or mine, will not remain constant, and we will probably drift apart. However, I know that she will always hold a big part of my heart, and I may one day look back on our friendship with wonder, awe and a smile. One day, I will be able to confidently call her one of my best friends and mean every sense of those words.

Loneliness and being alone does not have to be anyone's curse or burden. My relationship and friendship with Emily is proof that once you give up on your preconceived notions of what love, relationships, and soul mates are, you open yourself up to the world of possibilities for all of that, and happiness is within anyone's grasp. A soul mate is a person that is ideally suited to you, and that is what I have found in my crazy, lovable, fumbling Chinese girl. I know my life will not be the same without her.

Thanks to that friendship, my needs from a relationship are vastly different. Previously, a connection was supposed to complete me, to fulfill me and to validate me. Now, all I want is to be understood, to be comfortable and to be celebrated. Happiness and fulfillment can only come from you and not from someone else. All the friendships that I have fostered during my life have shown me love, loyalty and support. However, they have also demonstrated that when it comes to human relationships, nothing is every constant. And when you are dealing with something as inconstant as human relations, you can only ever look to yourself for contentment, happiness, and fulfilment.

Being other

"Knowing yourself is the beginning of all wisdom."

- ARISTOTLE

I met Christopher approximately six months after I first arrived in Bangkok. We met through mutual friends on a night that can only be described as 'epic.' We ate, drank, sang, danced till our feet bled and got along as if we had known each other all our lives. Christopher made me laugh till my eyes teared and my belly hurt – in my view, the best kind of people.

He was a good looking man, tall and lean with a mass of fiery red hair, deep dark brown eyes that sparkled with mischief, and alabaster white skin. Checking all the boxes that will make any lady look twice. However, his mannerisms and gestures yelled out gay. And that was all good with me, as I firmly believe every girl needs a 'gazband.'

A 'gazband' is a gay man who is more than just a best friend. A 'gazband' is the gay friend that accompanies you to the fancy gala dinner that your actual husband is never in the mood to attend. He is the man that you have dates with because your real husband or boyfriend can no longer be bothered to impress you and take you anywhere that is not his favourite sport's bar. A 'gazband' is your confidant, listens to your complaints, vents, and rants without interruption, and provides sound advice as feedback. Boyfriends and husbands should encourage this practice for every woman to find herself a 'gazband.' I think it would save many heterosexual relationships from impending doom or implosion.

After that first night, Christopher and I spent loads of crazy nights and weekends together. We became firm friends very quickly. The experiencing and acquiring of all things fun was first and foremost on the list. We sought out the hedonism that Bangkok nights offered, like addicts seek out their next high. Christopher was the male friend with whom I could go out on the town and have a drunken time of my life without having to worry about any consequences of losing control with him. With Christopher, I knew I was safe and could be whomever and did whatever I wanted. It was truly liberating to be in his company.

We often slept over at each other's apartments to make sure we got home safely and unscathed. The unspoken rule, yet one we followed religiously, was that no one goes back home alone and never with a stranger. We were young and carefree, not stupid and careless or naïve about how the world worked. The world can be a scary and dangerous place for a gay man and a single female.

Our shared hangovers were always severe and rendered us useless. However, the recollections of the night's antics and escapades would make us laugh till we gasped for air, snorted, and then just doubled over in a fit of laughter again.

After one such antic-filled night, we ended up staying at Christopher's apartment. It was about midday, and we were still in bed, trying to claw our way back to some semblance of normality from the revelries of the night before. We were also desperately trying to pry our tongues off the back of our palettes. There is no thirst like the drought a tequila hangover causes. Without a doubt, we looked exactly the way we felt – like crap.

We had just recovered from a fit of laughter after recalling an unfortunate incident involving Christopher, an imaginary cigarette, and a charming barman when he turned to me with his serious face. By this time, Christopher and I were together enough days and nights to know each other's expressions and what each one meant. We both suffered the fate of having no poker face; our emotions always transparent on our faces. So when I saw Christopher's sombre expression, I quickly sat up, straightened my spine, and readied myself for what was to come.

You may have the impression that every moment Christopher and I spent together entailed no more than moments of hedonism, drunkness and nightly delights, but that was not always the case. There were also much red wine and pizza-fuelled sofa nights where we just spoke about everything. We would discuss every topic under the sun, challenge each other's long-standing beliefs on almost every subject, and just vent about what we thought were unfair and undeserving situations and scenarios. We also shared a little bit about our pre-Bangkok lives and what our dreams are for the future.

Christopher turned to me and asked: "Nols," he never used my full name "what is the real reason you came to Bangkok?"

My initial thought was that it's bizarre this topic of conversation never came up before, quickly followed by wondering why Christopher felt the need to ask a deep and meaningful question like that now. We had spoken about our past before and briefly flipped on the reasons we ended up in Bangkok, but I could sense that that was not what he was asking. He wanted more; he needed to know about my introspection.

After a big sigh and a rapid decision to be completely honest, I said: "I am here to heal and learn to love myself." Christopher looked at me for what felt like an eternity and then slowly started nodding his head as if my answer confirmed what he was already thinking.

He dropped his chin to his chest, crossed his arms across his chest, gave a big sigh, and then said: "Me too. I am not myself yet. I am here learning to be me – the real me."

His voice and demeanour held the most profound sadness, but I could not figure out what he meant. Also, I was slightly confused as Christopher always seemed happy, satisfied, and confident. It was not the case. And I should have known better, the queen of sublimation herself.

We sat in silence for a while as I sensed that Christopher had not finished his story, he just needed time. After a few moments, he said: "Nols, I am going to tell you something that I've not told anyone; in fact, it's something I had only admitted to myself a year ago. Lots of people, honestly, everyone I know believes that I'm gay, but I'm not."

Again I just sat and waited, not knowing what was coming next. I braced myself for any possibility.

"I'm transgender," he finally said. For the first time in forever, I was utterly speechless, gobsmacked. There are no English words available to explain the confusion I felt accurately. All I could muster at the time was a very lame and drawn out, "Oh."

As I sat on the bed trying to wrap my head around this, Christopher went on to speak and explain as best he could.

"That is the real reason I came to Thailand. It is so that I can transition. So I can be complete. So I can start to live my life on my terms."

All this time, I sat silently listening and absorbing as best I could. Also, I felt that Christopher did not need me to say anything; he needed me to listen. To listen, to truly listen for understanding and not to respond, is often a significant element of friendship we all forget.

"I've been living as 'un-me' for so long, I feel like I can't breathe anymore." he continued. "I know what Atlas feels like, except my burden is not the world itself; rather, it's the weight of the world's judgment, prejudice, stereotyping, and fear. Other people's perception of how I should be has imprisoned me for as long as I can remember. I know many people think I am gay, but I'm not – never have been. My manner has always been feminine because that is who I am; that is how I feel. No, it is *who* I feel. I've been told by my family that when my mom was pregnant, everyone was convinced and believed completely that I was going to be a girl, but out came me instead. I don't think my family's senses where all that off though, I am a girl. A girl that has taken a longer path than most to get to that female state of being."

He finally lifted his head, uncrossed his arms, placed his hands in his lap, and with a big sigh, looked at me and said: "This is the quietest I've ever heard you. You've not spoken a word in over 15 minutes – that must be a record for you." He gave me the smallest and saddest smile I have ever seen.

I tried to snap out of my stunned stupor as best I could. I straightened up, snapped my mouth shut, cleared my throat, and said: "Well, I've always wanted a man to leave me speechless, but this is not quite what I had in mind. The universe got it horribly wrong."

Chris and I started howling with laughter; we could not contain ourselves. Rolling on the bed, snorting between breaths, then clutching our bellies and just laughing over and over again. It must have been a full 10 minutes of uncontrollable, tension relieving, belling aching laughter.

After our fit of giggles and laughs, we just laid side by side on the bed staring at the ceiling, completely exhausted. Christopher slowly turned his head to me and shyly asked: "What are your thoughts Nols? Now that you know who I truly am, are you disappointed?"

I quickly jumped off the bed without saying a word, stood at the side of the bed for a few seconds staring at him and ran to the kitchen. Christopher must have thought I was deserting him in his greatest hour of need, but I came back a few minutes later with two glasses filled to the brim with red wine.

I stood at the bedroom door and said: "Hey, it is after midday, and I think this calls for a toast, a celebration, and a plan for a shopping trip. 'Cause my new girlfriend is going to need some new clothes."

Christopher gave me the biggest smile. I passed him his glass, placed mine on the bedside table, and gave him the biggest hug I had the strength for and one that he could stand. I whispered in his ear: "I could never be disappointed with a soul as brave as yours, or with a person as courageous as you."

We picked up our glasses, and toasted to the start of a new life, celebrated friendship and acceptance. It was also the last time I ever referred to Christopher as he or even used that name.

That is how Christine's journey to womanhood started and how I met one of the bravest girls I know in Bangkok.

A few days after Christine told me that she is transgender, and the reason for her moving to Thailand, the next steps and months to come were a lot harder and even more eventful. First off, Christine knew she had to tell all her friends who she considered dear to her. Christine was acutely aware of the fact that she would lose some friends along the way as transgender or transexual people is still something many people do not, cannot accept or understand. She also had to tell her family.

Christine decided to confide in her friends first. The reason was two-fold. Firstly, so she could have a network of support around her should things go awry with her family. Secondly, to weed out all the nay-sayers, intolerants, and ones bent on hate. Having that network of support is vital to any female trying to get ahead in this world. Even more so for lesbians, transgender and transsexuals. A self-created support network is always there to help us go through whatever problem we may face at one time or another.

At the time, the biggest hurdle to telling her family was the fact that they lived in Africa. She put it off for the longest time, and I was in no way going to force her. The reveal to her family had to be on her terms and her time. All I could do was offer support for whatever happened after.

Sometimes, that is all we can do as friends. Listen, support, comfort but never dictate, never convey advice unless asked, and never assume that your way is the right way. Luckily for me and bravely for Christine, it was a few weeks after she and I had our moment that she had a Skype chat with her family.

I was not there to witness the event. I believed that she would need the space to tell her family her way, without any silent pressure from me. I requested that she call me after the event, and I would be right over. I only lived a 10-minute ride away, so I could be there in a jiffy whenever she needed me.

I can only guess at how the events played out during that Skype chat. Christine must have been going through every emotion from one second to the next. She was a nervous wreck during the time to the run-up to the call. I was anxiously pacing and continuously glancing at my wall clock in the apartment. After lots of coffee and cigarettes for me, she called at 10 pm. I answered the call, but all the while holding my breath for whatever was going to come next. What happened next was a pleasant surprise. After my cautious 'Hello,' I said, "And. .?" leaving the question hanging on the line between us.

After an eternity, or rather what felt like an eternity, Christine let out a long sigh and said: "I'm OK, Nols. It went well. Very well, actually."

I was both stupefied with relief and overwhelmed with pure happiness to hear that.

"I take it they accepted what you had to say and who you are without a qualm?" I asked.

"Yes, they did. It was surreal. Every worst-case scenario I built up in my head did not happen. All they said was that they understood and that they always suspected. My family thought I was gay and suspected the Skype call was me finally coming out." she said with a nervous giggle.

She went on to say: "Well, I did come out, and my family did admit that my reveal was a bit of a surprise. But ultimately, they just want me to be happy and to be who I am meant to be."

After hearing that, I immediately fell in love with Christine's family. How many of us know people that have come out to their families and were then cast out, shunned and disowned. Here was Christine, not only telling her family what they suspected but telling them that she was not who they have raised, nurtured, cared for, and thoroughly believed they fully knew and understood.

The unconditional acceptance by Christine's family was simply amazing for me, and I knew that she came from a strong and resilient family. She came from good stock, and she would need that strength for the journey ahead. The sort of empathy and understanding displayed by Christine's mom and dad is a truly beautiful thing. Perhaps that comes with being a great parent – I have no idea. All I know is, Christine's family became my instant heroes.

Christine and I did not chat very long that night. She, understandably, was emotionally drained. I was physically exhausted due to hours of pent up anxiety and worry. We both called it an early night and made a tentative date to take Christine out in public for the first time.

It was three days after her Skype call with her family that Christine and I saw each other. The plan was to get her dress and be the lady she feels finally. My job was that of a wardrobe coordinator. I can't say it was due to my impeccable taste; I simply had more practice time than her. She had already managed to buy some blouses, some trousers, as she was not confident enough to wear a dress or a skirt yet, and shoes, as well as makeup and accessories.

We had so much fun putting her outfit together and doing her makeup. It was terrific to watch Christine go through all of these experiences for the first time. The rites of passage to womanhood that we get to learn and experience during our formative and teenage years, she had to learn in a few days and months. She handled it all incredibly well and took to it like a duck to water. There is little doubt that these days

Christine has way more makeup skills than I do. What she can do with a bit of concealer, foundation and shadows are amazing.

Once we got her dressed and accessorised, it was ready to hit the town. Well, not exactly a night like we were used to, the plan was to go to a food court situated a mere five minutes up the road from her apartment. The aim was not to go out and have a wild night on the town; it was to get Christine comfortable in her new skin.

The food courts in Bangkok are always a hive of activity and bustle of people. Also, a great night of food for very little money. Anyone who knows me well will know that food courts are my idea of the perfect food place – inexpensive, plentiful, and provide many hours of excellent people-watching opportunities.

Christine stood in the middle of her living room, and I had my hand on the doorknob.

Ready?" I asked.

"Yes!" she confidently replied.

As I opened the door, she just crumbled into a quivering mess. Christine was a wreck of nerves. She took her handbag off her shoulder and sat down on the sofa.

"Just a seccie Nols. I need a little more time, " she said while sitting on the sofa, all the while shaking like a leaf.

In no way was I going to rush this. I didn't say a word. I closed the door, put my bag on the floor, walked over to the fridge, and got out two beers. As I wordlessly handed Christine her beer, I sagged down on the sofa next to her. As I sat slouched against the backrest of the couch, I watched my dear friend go through one of the biggest agonies in her life.

Just before I took a sip of my beer, I said: "When you are ready, honey. I have all night and a fridge full of beers. I don't need to go anywhere, and pizza is a phone call away when we get hungry."

She turned to face me and gave me a sheepish smile. We clinked our beer bottles as a way of acknowledging and just sat in silence.

It took me three hours and lots of beer to get Christine to the elevator. It took encouragement and loads of back rubbing to get her out of the elevator. Once out of the apartment, it took constant words of encouragement and support, such as: "You made it this far. Why not a bit more?" over a hundred times to get her to the food court.

Anyone could see that Christine was a bundle of nerves during our walk to the food court. She was constantly adjusting her clothes, even though there was nothing amiss. Her hands constantly and feverishly sought out something to do, to adjust clothing, hair or earring, to cling to on her person. Halfway into our walk, I realised my constant affirmations were falling on deaf ears.

When we got to the food court, Christine felt everyone's eyes on her. She kept nervously touching her hair or readjusting her clothes. At this stage, I was not overly concerned about Christine's discomfort; I was wholly absorbed by a beer-fuelled hunger that demanded immediate attention.

We got our favourite dishes. I knew she needed as much of the familiar as possible, and comfort food always helps in stressful times. I was ravenously devouring my plate, but Christine barely touched her favourite meal. Eventually, after the hunger monster stopped tearing me up from the inside. I sat back and looked at Christine. Her eyes were darting everywhere, but not looking for anything or anyone, in particular, it was her way of keeping herself pre-occupied and not focused on the people around her.

I eventually couldn't hold my tongue and said: "Would you relax. No one is looking at you. It is all in your head."

She stopped fidgeting, and the squirrel-eye darting for a second to look at me and said, "I can't help it, Nols. I feel as if everyone is staring at me."

I tossed my napkin in my empty plate, leaned forward, and said to her: "OK! The next person who looks at you – show me, so we can both smile and wave at them. Let's make your discomfort theirs to deal with."

Christine bowed her head and patted the back of her hair down. When she flipped her head back up, she said: "OK, fine, let's try that."

We sat in the food court a bit longer. All the while, I was asking her about work and how she found that blouse. Just trying to have girl-talk with her. All of a sudden, Christine's head darted my way and said: "There's one!"

I looked in the direction she was gesturing and true to her word; a man was staring at her. I motioned for her to follow my lead. We both turned our chairs to face him, smiled seductively, and waved at him. The poor man did not know where to look after that. We caught him completely off-guard.

Christine and I burst out laughing. We gave each other a high five. I turned to her and asked, "Who was more uncomfortable right now? You or him?"

"Absolutely him," she said, still giggling nervously.

"Exactly," I said, "use your uniqueness to your advantage. Show these narrow-minded fools for exactly what they are. Never feel ashamed of who you are. They should be the ones to feel shame for their ignorance. Love and live who are you, my beautiful Christine. You deserve it. To hell with these idiots."

"Yes! To hell with the whole lot of them. They are not important – I am" she said.

With that, we got up and headed back to the apartment. This time without any coaxing or encouragement from me. Christine left that food court like a calm, collected and mature woman. It was truly amazing to see. She transformed into a calm, confident, and mature woman in a matter of hours. Some women I know take a lifetime to reach the same level of confidence I saw in Christine.

Christine is one of the lucky ones who has not experienced any ignorance or intolerance from her family or friends. She has also been fortunate to have found an online job that does not require her to go into an office of starring eyes every day. Not every transgender or transsexual person is as lucky as Christine. However, in no way does that distract from Christine's bravery and courage that is on display every day from other people who feel themselves the standard-bearers for everything righteous and proper in this world.

Christine has learned over the last few years to deal with intolerance from outside her support network. Others, not as lucky as her, have to learn to fight or be fast for the flight.

My admiration and respect for her grow every day I know

Christine. She is still one of the bravest ladies I have met in Bangkok.

To Tinder, or not to Tinder...that is the question.

"Everything in the world is about sex except sex. Sex is about power."
- **OSCAR WILDE**

You would be hard-pressed to find a single person in Bangkok who has not flirted with online dating. Most single people in Bangkok use a dating app, or two, or a few. In a city where most foreigners are passing through, you are spoilt for app options and choices within. In Bangkok, men have a plethora of opportunities for women who cater to every man's taste and desire. Women these days have their fair choice too.

Dating was the topic of conversation around the post-dinner table one Saturday evening on a girl's night out. There were the usual suspects that I hung out with most weekends; no one was unfamiliar to each other, so the conversation and the wine flowed freely. There were no holds barred confessions and stories that would make some porn stars cringe.

In one instance, Bethany was regaling us with a tale about a horrendous meetup. A guy she met online and who she finally agreed to meet face-to-face. Bethany admitted that there was something off about him, but she could not pinpoint precisely what it was via the numerous text messages they exchanged. After weeks of to-ing and fro-ing, she eventually agreed to meet for drinks. Beth decided on a familiar venue – just in case a quick getaway was needed.

She mentioned that he was good looking and luckily matched his profile picture, so first off, there was no cause for alarm. She described him as looking like John Mayer with less charisma and way more hair product. So, again, no horrible surprises. However, through the entire evening, something was off; he was just trying too hard. He spoke too fast, made ridiculous and outrageous statements. Tried to be funny and failed miserably every time. At no time was he rude, crude or repulsive, but something was niggling her and just couldn't figure what. Bethany had a great sense of humour, but she had to admit that this guy was pushing the boundaries way too much. His sense of humour just made her feel uncomfortable, but she still smiled and giggled politely.

Bethany loathed to admit it, but after a few margaritas, she ended up riding the elevator in the hotel to his room. She had doubts in the taxi, doubts on the way to the hotel, all the way on the elevator and even once she was in his room. However, alcohol-fuelled bravado and lack of inhibitions do not allow for sound decision making. She didn't feel unsafe with him; something just felt off.

In his room, things heated up quickly. A good kisser and good hands that knew where to go and what to do once they got there. However, once they were naked and on the bed, he became almost manic. The man was all over the place. Bethany described his sexual techniques as trying to fit every porno scene he had ever watched into two hours. She didn't know what was going on half the time. To say the sex was unsatisfactory would have been an understatement, she explained. She was exhausted by the end of it, but that was solely down to her just trying to keep up with all his moves. It felt more like a workout than an erotic interlude. While she described what was going on in that hotel room, the people seated at the table were crying with laughter. Half of it we couldn't believe.

Eventually, after the mirth had died down, someone asked, "So what was the thing that wasn't quite right about this guy – besides the obvious? Did you ever find out, or was that it?"

Bethany went on to tell us that after the unsatisfactory sheet-tussle, the two of them started to chat about everyday things. However, again this guy couldn't sit still for longer than five minutes. She thought perhaps he was a coke head, as he displayed all the classic signs. However, that wasn't it, she sensed something else, and it still niggled her. While she was gathering her things to leave, she thought she would throw out a question to settle her curiosity. She point-blank asked him if he was married. She could see him wrestle with his conscience for a few seconds before he admitted that he was.

For Bethany, the entire evening's craziness just suddenly all made sense. She told us that she sat down and asked him why he did this to his wife, why did he feel the need to cheat, why not just leave? Again, alcohol consumption and one night stands do not make for sound judgement calls, she readily admitted. He admitted to her that it was his first time at cheating or being with another woman and Beth believed him. No man who was accustomed to lying would be that bad at picking up a woman, or that terrible at no strings attached sex. They continued to talk long into the night, and she eventually left his hotel room the next morning – without any further forays into sex. He explained what was happening in his life, and Beth sat and listened. She didn't judge, didn't cast aspersions, and offered no advice. He piqued her curiosity.

Beth went onto say that when it came time for her to leave, he gave her a strong and deep hug and whispered, "Thank you." When Beth asked him what for, he said that he hadn't felt this good in a long time, and it had nothing to do with the sex, it was just her presence and her willingness to listen that made him feel lighter and more positive. He also apologised for the terrible sex. Beth said that they still keep in touch and he is getting on with his life as best he can, and admits that he no longer explores into the world of one night stands.

Beth said, "I firmly believe a woman who finds herself with a married man cannot say that she doesn't know. There is always something that gives you a little niggle, a sense that something is off, or little things that just don't add up - women know." She has never again ignored that niggle and never again gone on a date or met up with a man she senses to be married.

On and on the stories went that night. The restaurant had long closed, but luckily for us, we knew the owner and were allowed to stay. Once the restaurant had closed, and all the staff had left, the owner joined us. The drinks kept flowing, the stories kept coming, and the laughter, shock and sometimes horror never stopped.

There was the story from Robyn, who was convinced a one night stand wanted to turn her into a pretzel. We all howled with laughter when she started telling us the story of how she was trying to figure out her missing nail polish from her big toe the next day. She remembers being at work and looking at her foot, finally noticing that there was a line of red polish missing from her right big toe. She had to admit to herself that she had a lot to drink but in no way drunk to the point where she couldn't recall knocking her toe or having someone step on her foot. She didn't remember any calamity that may have resulted in her missing nail varnish. She went about the rest of her day and forgot about the nail varnish mystery. When she got home, she got on with the chore of cleaning up before settling down for the evening and recuperating from the night-before shenanigans. She was making her bed when she spotted a red line across the wall over her bed.

"How the hell did that get there?" she recalls wondering to herself. When suddenly, all the yoga-like techniques of the night before came flooding back and she could not believe she was able to do half of those positions. She recalled dissolving into a fit of laughter when she realised how that streak of red came to be on her bedroom wall. Up to this day, she still calls him Mr Pretzel, a fact of which he is well aware. They are good friends today and always share a good laugh about the night they met.

There was a story from Bron who had dinner with the perfect gentleman, who did everything right until he tried to convince her to have a threesome with him and his sister. The stories indeed ranged from the ridiculous to the outrageous, from the weird to the wonderful and from the embarrassing to the cringe-worthy.

There was one great story from Mel who met her husband on Tinder. They were just lucky she surmised as they both took a chance, and it turned out to be a good call. Initially, she had skipped his profile three times before deciding to like him based purely on the fact that he kept popping back into her feed. After weeks of exchanging text, it became clear to both of them that they liked each other and had heaps in common. When Mel did meet up with the guy, she was pleased to see that he looked like his profile picture and it was all genuine. He was indeed a good guy with a great personality and a physical frame she could play monkey bars on for a few hours. They dated for a few months and decided to get married after a short drunken conversation. The next day they both made sure the other still remembered the conversation and that they still wanted the same thing. They were married three months later. That girl's night, Mel was married for a year, and they were still going strong and very much in love. She and her husband had both been living in Bangkok for two years as single people by the time they had met. Bangkok has become their home, and they plan on living and raising a family in the city they love.

There was also Sally who met the man of her dreams and had a whirlwind three-week romance with him. It was terrific, and she believes that they would have made a fantastic team - had he stayed in Bangkok.

Things were heating up, and conversations started heading in the direction of a full-blown relationship. The sort of conversations that leads you to change your profile status delete all the dating apps off your phone and makes you smile like an idiot all day. However, the company that the gentleman in question worked for decided that his skill set was best suited for a different part of the globe, and he got shipped off to India. Sure, he could have stayed in Bangkok, but that meant he had to leave a job he loved and one that gave him an incredible life. Sally would never have asked him to do either.

Also, Sally could have gone to India, but the relationship was too young to decide about a life-changing moment that large. Everyone around the table agreed with Sally that you could not base a massive decision like that on what you want without having some in-depth and meaningful conversations. They hadn't even decided if they were in a full-blown relationship yet. So, with a heavy heart, Sally bid her potential happily-ever-after farewell and still hopes that one day they are offered a charge to rekindle and explore the potential of a great partnership. She explained that they are still in touch but leading very separate and different lives. As she summed it up, "Perhaps not today, but maybe one day."

I am fully aware that there will be people reading this thinking these women to be loose, cheap, and 'easy' and all the usual slurs that get thrown around when it comes to women expressing and owning their sexuality. The "old boys' club of chasing skirts and sowing their seed will cast aspersions and slurs that these women are no good. However, nothing is further from the truth. These days, women are taking back the power, which has, for so many generations, been denied to them. Women all over the world are saying 'no more' to the patriarchal system of controlling female sexuality, women's bodies and personal choices.

These women who I sat around a table with, drinking and sharing, are not lost, crazy, cheap, prostitutes, or 'easy'. They are intelligent, successful, independent and balanced individuals who want to share and celebrate themselves with someone. With someone who enjoys them, recognise their 'awesome' and is not be threatened by their strength and self-expression. These are women who played the game set out by antiquated societal norms for years and continuously lost, or were left with little dignity intact. These girls, or rather women, who I met in Bangkok, were owning their sexuality, determining the terms of how these encounters happen and trying to find an equal footing in the relationship game.

In the City of angels, women are learning to love themselves, appreciate men, and take an equal part in developing a meaningful and valued partnership with someone. They are indeed loving, living and thriving in Bangkok.

We are warriors

"The only people who get upset about you setting boundaries are the ones who were benefiting from you having none."

-   ANONYMOUS

"My story is no different from the rest. Only the details differ," said Moira in answer to a question from one of the group. A small group of girlfriends decided to meet for sundowners on the Chao Praya River. We had tasty cocktails, a great view of Wat Arun, and a sunset that painted the sky with hues of red, pink, lavender and purple.

As the evening cooled, the conversation heated up. An innocent vent by one of the group regarding her boyfriend's inattentiveness escalated to a debate about why people, but men, in particular, abuse. There was a distinct grouping among us ladies. One part of the group believed that it wasn't a choice for them as it was more about conditioning or experiences of abuse. The other part of the group firmly believed that abusers choose to become that by their words and actions.

The fact that this topic so polarised the group was not surprising. Psychologists and psychiatrists have tried for decades to answer the same question with very little success. The surprise came in the fact that every single one of us sitting at that table experienced abuse of some form at the hands of people we trusted. Every single one of us, from every corner of the globe and very different social backgrounds, experienced some form of physical, emotional, mental or sexual abuse. That fact shocked us into a few seconds of silence when one of the group pointed out that fact to all.

Moira started telling us her story of survival. She lived through a three-year relationship littered with abuse. "He wasn't like that in the beginning. The first year he was amazing, everything you could want from a partner. However, that all changed when we decided to live together."

"I'm embarrassed to tell you my story because of how cliché it is. First, he is an amazing guy, then the controlling starts. Later, he takes away all your personal and physical comforts, then when you are truly at his mercy, he becomes the monster. We have all heard this story before, and we all think to ourselves that it will never happen to us. We know the signs, we read all the articles that tell us to look for the signs, to be aware, but we never see them. The signs slip past in apologies, remorse, and makeups", she said.

Moira went on to tell us how her boyfriend physically abused her for two years. The breaking point for her came with a moment during a beating where he tried to bite off her nose. She was in the hospital for days and needed reconstructive surgery to fix the damage he had done to her nose. She refused contact with him, and the hospital staff was well aware that he was no allowed anywhere near her. The police were useless and of absolutely no help. "Get a restraining order," was all the advice given. "How is a restraining order going to help when his fists are beating me to death?" she questioned. "Do I shove the restraining order in his face while he is trying to squeeze my life out my throat? Bloody useless the whole legal system," she went on to vent. After discharging herself from the hospital, she drove straight to her friend's house and lived there until the day she moved to Bangkok.

"I never went home for anything. Not my belongings, not even my clothes. I sent some of my friends to get some things for me later down the line, but I made up my mind the day I left the hospital that I didn't want to see, hear, feel or breathe the same air as that monster. My gut told me that the next time I would not survive it. His beatings escalated over the years, and I wasn't going to wait around for him to kill me."

The way Moira told her story made her ordeal sound like something normal. She told us in the same tone as if she was telling us about her trip to the store. It was a bit eerie, but understandable by all around the table. We all know that when you don't detach yourself from it in a healthy way, you end up reliving it every day as if you are still in the moment. She went on to tell us that after six months on her friend's sofa, she realised she needed to change the dynamic. Living with the monster was going to kill her, but going on the way she was– existing and not living was going to kill her soul. After some research and job searching, she chose Thailand for its beautiful beaches, never-ending summer, and most importantly, for the distance.

"I bought a plane ticket, packed up my little belongings, said goodbye to all those that supported me even after I threw them away, and came to start a new life. I came here to live and live I have," she said.

Moira was right, and her story is not that different from anyone who has ever lived through abuse. We start out hating ourselves, blaming ourselves, and chastising ourselves for allowing it to happen. A switch flips and then you realise who is actually at fault, and it's not you. Monsters come in all shapes and sizes of the human form. Once you met one and lived through their evil deeds, you focus on life. For most of us around that table, the abuse we experienced left us all with the highest resolution never to let it happen again and never to give our monsters the satisfaction to know they affect or affected us in any way.

We have all heard various forms of these stories. Not only stories that reflect Moira's, but there are also the stories that echo Brit's who was sexually abused by a close family friend from the age of nine. It carried on until she was sixteen years old. There is the story of Nan, whose mother saw it fit to project all her discontent on her daughter. Nan grew up told she is not worth anything, that she is unintelligent and a loser just like her absent father.

"When you are told something long enough, you start believing it. Every negative word my mother launched at me, I started living. I became exactly what she told me I was. One day after waking up in the hospital, having no recollection of how I got there, I knew something had to change," said Nan. "I remember the nursing staff telling me I was brought in with enough alcohol and drugs in my system to knock out an elephant. If someone didn't pick me up from the street and bring me in, I would certainly have died. I went home after hospital but not one kind word from the woman who was supposed to love me more than anyone else in this world. I packed a bag and went into rehab. Six years later, I'm still sober and a successful businesswoman. I assume my mother is still consumed in her anger because I've not seen or spoken to her in six years. I don't see that changing anytime soon."

There is the story of Linda, who was stalked and terrorised by someone who assumed he was entitled to her body, mind, and heart-based purely on the fact that she was kind to him. Linda had to flee her home country to lose her stalker. The police and the justice system were unable to help her as she experienced no physical harm. It is unbelievable how justice systems around the world have been so slow in changing antiquated laws that do nothing to protect women. Linda had to give up her life, career and leave her family because someone thought it his right to her based purely on the fact that he believed he was entitled to it all.

"I went on one date with this psycho," she explained. "The date wasn't all that great. He was pleasant enough company but nothing else. I didn't want to be horrid and never really told him I wasn't interested, but every time a suggestion of a second date came up, I would either ignore it or come up with an excuse. He was doggedly determined and eventually, I couldn't avoid it any longer. I told him that I am not interested in dating or seeing anyone right now, and he lost it. He called me a cock tease, a whore and a gold-digger. I was shocked and let him vent thinking if he just got it out of his system and he would leave me alone. Boy, I was mistaken. This guy kept texting, calling and showing up at my place. He even followed me to work. Then the threats started. First, he was going to get me evicted, then fired, and then he threatened to harm me. I went to the police, filed the necessary papers but that didn't deter him in any way. I lived with friends, moved around the city, but he didn't stop. After two years of this, I knew that I was either going to go crazy, he was going to harm me, or I would be dead. I hated living with that constant fear and anxiety. I knew I had to leave, so I packed a suitcase and came to Thailand."

"Are you not scared he will follow you here?" I asked.

"Yes, for a long time after I arrived here, I would still look over my shoulder every five minutes. I would still jump every time my phone rang or when I heard a loud noise. I instantly panicked every time I saw someone who vaguely resembled him. The slightest whiff of his cologne would set off my anxiety. It took time, but I eventually started feeling normal. It has been five years, and I've not heard anything from him. The thing is, when I left, I told no one I was leaving. I just picked up what I could and left. When I got here, I called my family, so he has no idea where I am, and my family knows not to say anything to anyone about my whereabouts."

Of all the stories told that night, the one similarity running through all of them is that we all survived. Whether it was physical, mental, sexual, or emotional, we all survived and came out better from it. Scarred yes, but better, wiser and stronger.

Here are a few other observations from our group of survivors we made that night. All of us do not accept apologies at face value. Everyone around that table agreed that an apology verbalised is empty without changed behaviour and we all now take the behaviour as an act of apology and remorse, not the empty words.

We are not jaded but overly cautious about opening up to people. Relationships are hard, not because we are demanding. Instead, our challenging nature stems from our partners not understanding the level of honesty we require or the deep-set mistrust we all carry.

Our bullshit meters are highly sensitive, so we don't do small talk very well. Most people who meet survivors for the first time think we are anti-social, but we just prefer to have meaningful conversations. It helps us gauge who you are. That doesn't mean we don't let our hair down and take turns at being the life of the party; we merely prefer to be that around people we trust.

We push ourselves harder to accomplish; we strive to achieve as much as we can. It is our way of telling the monsters that they didn't win. They didn't break us.

All of us care, really care for each other and other people. We know how it is to suffer personally and we will never see anyone else in a similar situation. We will all help when and where we can, especially women and children who need it the most. I recall briefly mentioning that night that we should consider forming a foundation for anyone needing to get out of a bad situation. We were going to call ourselves the 'Born,

Bred, and Fleds.' It never happened, of course, but not an entirely bad idea. Perhaps I may still do it to honour these women I call friends and to pay tribute to their struggles, trials and tribulations.

Just like warriors, of past and present, we have fought our battles. Returned from those battles bloodied, broken, and damaged. Fighting your internal demons after the battle is the longest and hardest road to recovery. Exorcising the guilt, banishing the self-blame and halting the self-loathing is a lonely path that only a fellow warrior will recognise. Forgiveness is a rock you have to learn how to swallow and with much practice and support you do eventually get there. However, those steps to forgiveness can never be taken alone. You need your army of warriors around you. Other battle-hardened women are the best mentors on your path to forgiveness. Be sure you seek them out.

I am not sure if it was a more profound recognition of an injured soul that brought me to these ladies or the city of Bangkok weaving its magic to bring us together. I do know that it has been great to know them and to navigate this amazing city together. A city that has once again allowed us to love, live, and thrive.

Upcoming publication from Noleen C. George

Arai Wa!
Kindness cost nothing but sometimes it takes away
everything.

Beth couldn't believe how an act of kindness could turn into
the one of the worst times of her life. Narcissism was always
something she heard about until she experienced the full
force of its negativity.

Follow the story of Beth who went from kind to vengeful
because of the mindless actions of one person.